THE
VELVETEEN
RABBIT

A Little Apple Classic

by Margery Williams Bianco
Illustrated by Charles Santore

KENNEBUNKPORT, MAINE

The Velveteen Rabbit: A Little Apple Classic

13-Digit ISBN: 978-1-60433-950-5
10-Digit ISBN: 1-60433-950-0

This book may be ordered by mail from the publisher.
Please include $5.95 for postage and handling.
Please support your local bookseller first!

Books published by Cider Mill Press Book Publishers are available at special discounts for bulk purchases in the United States by corporations, institutions, and other organizations. For more information, please contact the publisher.

Applesauce Press is an imprint of
Cider Mill Press Book Publishers
"Where Good Books Are Ready for Press"
PO Box 454
12 Spring Street
Kennebunkport, Maine 04046

Visit us online at:
www.cidermillpress.com

Typography: Adobe Caslon Pro and ITC Caslon
Printed in China

3 4 5 6 7 8 9 0

THERE WAS ONCE

a Velveteen Rabbit, and in the
beginning he was really splendid.
He was fat and bunchy, as a rabbit
should be; his coat was spotted
brown and white, and his ears
were lined with pink sateen.

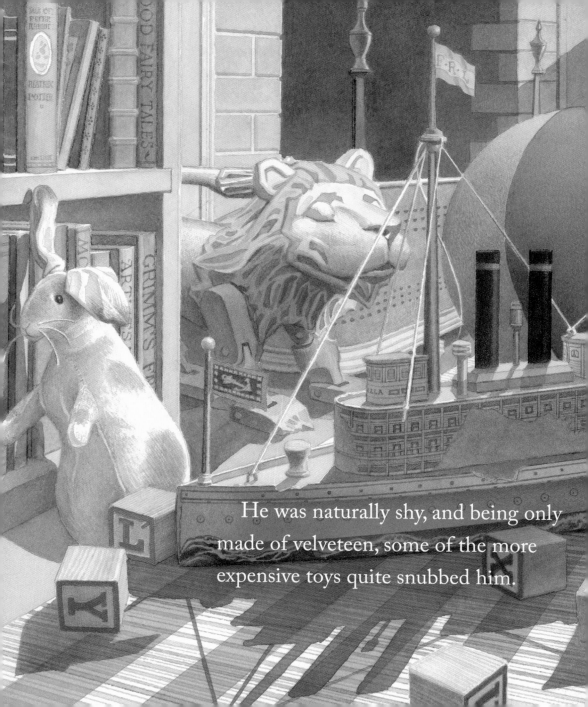

He was naturally shy, and being only made of velveteen, some of the more expensive toys quite snubbed him.

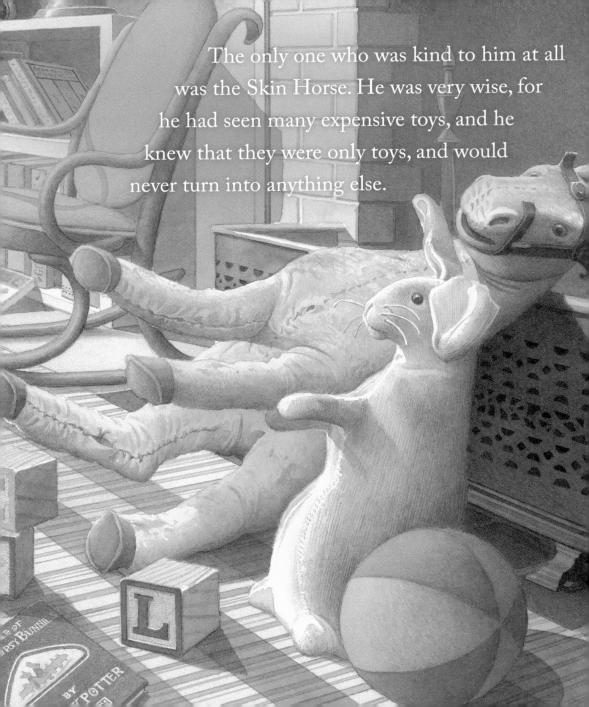

The only one who was kind to him at all was the Skin Horse. He was very wise, for he had seen many expensive toys, and he knew that they were only toys, and would never turn into anything else.

"What is REAL?" asked the Rabbit one day.

"Real isn't how you're made," said the Skin Horse. "It's a thing that happens to you when a child loves you for a long time. By the time you are Real, you get loose in the joints and very shabby. But once you are Real, you can't be ugly, except to people who don't understand."

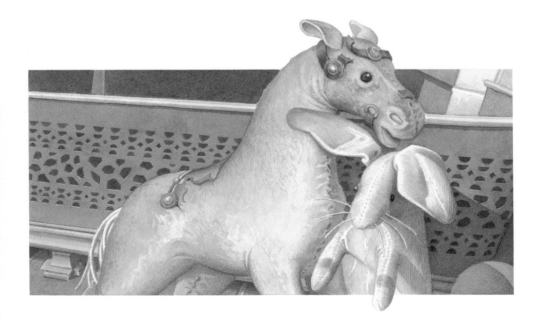

One evening, when the Boy was going to bed, he couldn't find the China Dog that always slept with him.

"Here," his Nana said, "take your old Bunny!"

That night, and for many nights after, the Velveteen Rabbit slept in the Boy's bed.

And so time went on, and the little Rabbit was very happy—so happy that he never noticed how his beautiful, velveteen fur was getting shabbier, and his tail was becoming unsewn, and all the pink rubbed off his nose where the Boy had kissed him.

Once, the Rabbit was left out after dusk, and Nana had to look for him because the Boy couldn't go to sleep unless he was there. "Fancy all that fuss for a toy!" she said.

"You mustn't say that," the Boy said. "He isn't a toy. He's REAL!"

When the little Rabbit heard that he was happy,
for he knew that what the Skin Horse had said
was true at last. He was Real. The Boy himself
had said it.

Near the house was a wood. One evening, while the Rabbit was lying there alone, he saw two strange beings. They were rabbits like himself, but quite furry and brand-new. They stared at him, and the little Rabbit stared back. And all the time their noses twitched.

"He hasn't got any hind legs! He doesn't smell right!" the wild rabbits exclaimed, jumping back. "He isn't a rabbit at all! He isn't real!"

"I am Real!" said the little Rabbit. "The Boy said so! Come back and play with me! I *know* I am Real!" But there was no answer.

Weeks passed, and the little Rabbit grew very old and shabby, but the Boy loved him just as much. He loved him so hard that the pink lining to his ears turned grey, and his brown spots faded.

And then, one day, the Boy was ill.

His little body was so hot it burned the Rabbit when he held him close. The Velveteen Rabbit lay there, hidden from sight under the bedclothes, for he was afraid that someone might take him away, and he knew that the Boy needed him.

Presently, the Boy got better. The room
was to be disinfected, and all the books and
toys that the Boy had played with in bed
must be burnt.

"How about his old Bunny?" Nana asked.

"*That?*" said the doctor. "Why, it's a mess
of germs! Burn it at once."

And so the little Rabbit was put into a sack and carried out to the garden. The little Rabbit felt very lonely. A tear, a real tear, trickled down his little, shabby, velvet nose and fell to the ground.

Where the tear had fallen, a flower grew out of the ground.

The blossom opened, and out of it stepped a fairy.

"I am the Nursery Magic Fairy," she said. "I take care of all the playthings that the children have loved. When they are old and worn out, I turn them Real."

"Wasn't I Real before?" asked the little Rabbit.

"You were Real to the Boy," the Fairy said, "because he loved you. Now you shall be Real to everyone."

She flew with the little Rabbit into the woods where the wild rabbits danced.

"I've brought you a new playfellow," the Fairy said. "You must be very kind to him and teach him all he needs to know in Rabbit Land."

And she kissed the little Rabbit again and put him down on the grass.

But the little Rabbit sat quite still for a moment, for he didn't want them to see that he was made all in one piece. He did not know that the Fairy had changed him. Just then, something tickled his nose, and before he thought what he was doing he lifted one of his hind legs to scratch it.

He actually had hind legs! Instead of dingy velveteen he had soft and shiny fur. He was a Real Rabbit at last.

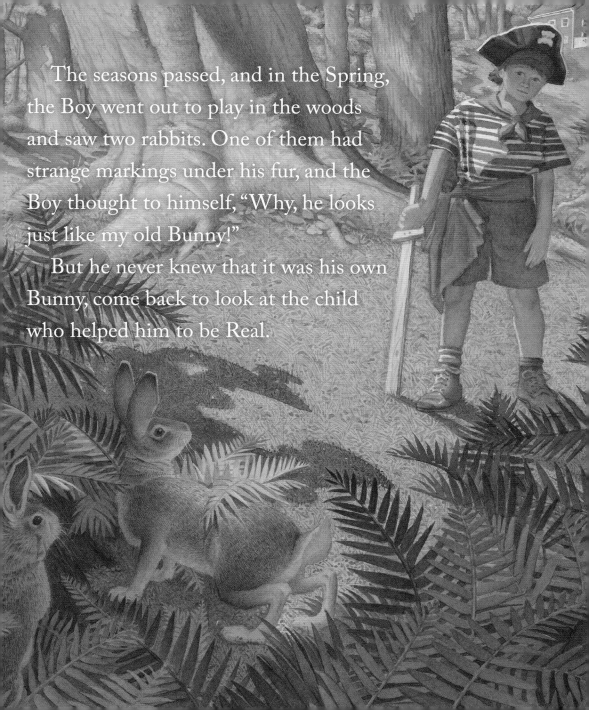

The seasons passed, and in the Spring, the Boy went out to play in the woods and saw two rabbits. One of them had strange markings under his fur, and the Boy thought to himself, "Why, he looks just like my old Bunny!"

But he never knew that it was his own Bunny, come back to look at the child who helped him to be Real.

About Applesauce Press

Good ideas ripen with time. From seed to harvest, Applesauce Press crafts books with beautiful designs, creative formats, and kid-friendly information on a variety of fascinating topics. Like our parent company, Cider Mill Press Book Publishers, our press bears fruit twice a year, publishing a new crop of titles each spring and fall.

Write to us at:
PO Box 454
Kennebunkport, ME 04046

Or visit us online at:
www.cidermillpress.com